A Present for Santa

Written & Illustrated by

Andrew Hirst

For Ruby... The most precious of all gems!

A new Christmas was on its way,
Harrison was jumping up and down,

but soon his thoughts turned to presents
and it was followed with a frown.

If Santa brings our presents and
leaves the Christmas cheer,

who will make the journey to leave something
for him this year?

The Easter Bunny would be painting eggs
with extra special care,

and the Tooth Fairy was always busy
combing money from her hair.

It was no good, the time had come,
an adventure must be had,

Harrison couldn't let Santa's Christmas morning
turn out to be that sad.

He packed up teddy, donned his boots
and a nice warm bobble hat,

and off he set, the North Pole he'd go,
before the goose had got too fat!

Goosey skqwarked and
away they flew above
roof tops and the trees,

North they shot and
good time they made
swooshing on the breeze.

NEEDLES INCLUDED

KNIT YOUR OWN
SOCKS
THE CRAFTY WAY TO KEEP YOUR FEET WARM

5+ £1.99

But then he saw it....
it was perfect he'd make it on the way,
he'd knit some socks so Father Christmas
would have a cosy Christmas Day.

The deal was done and all set with needles and some wool,
back in the air and North they flew over Istanbul.
They flew past by Paris and New York,
maybe Goosey's get-ting lost,

but then Harrison knew they
were nearly there because his
ears were full of frost!

North Pole ahoy, the chimney loomed,
they landed with a bump,

on the roof they were quite high and
much too far to jump!

The present was wrapped badly but it didn't matter none, as Harrison was just excited about all this Christmas fun.

ZZZ
HO HO HO... you've both been very good this year...
To TED Love Santa xx

Printed in Poland
by Amazon Fulfillment
Poland Sp. z o.o., Wrocław